W9-CCS-176

CAVEMAN

A B.C. STORY

CAVEMAN A.B.C. STORY

BY JANEE TRASLER

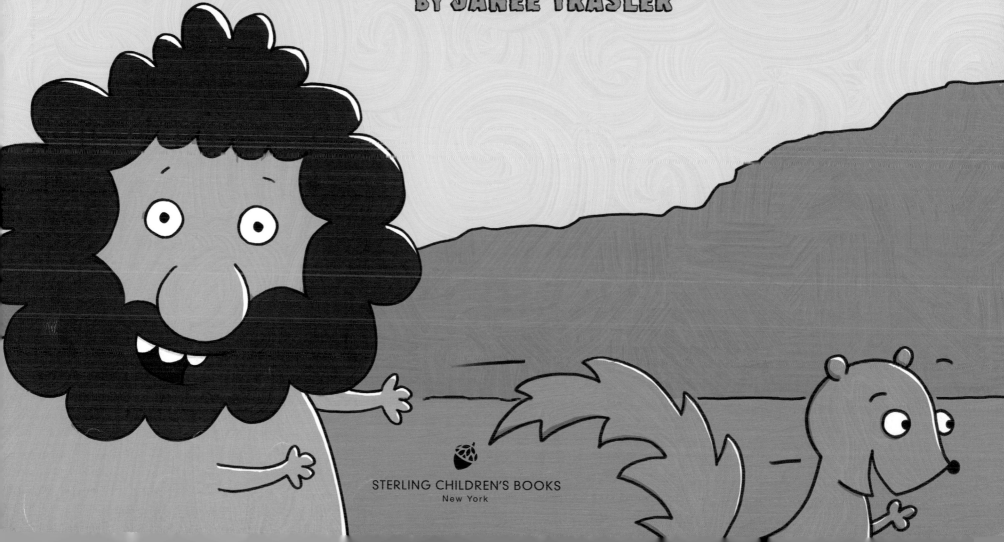

STERLING CHILDREN'S BOOKS

New York

TREE

UM...

Zzzz...

FOR LEIGH

STERLING CHILDREN'S BOOKS
New York

An Imprint of Sterling Publishing
387 Park Avenue South
New York, NY 10016

STERLING and the distinctive Sterling logo are registered trademarks of
Sterling Publishing Co., Inc.

Library of Congress Cataloging-in-Publication Data
Trasler, Janee.
Caveman : a B. C. story / Janee Trasler.
p. cm.
Summary: Illustrations and twenty-six simple words introduce the alphabet
through the adventures of a cave man.
ISBN 978-1-4027-7119-4 (hc-plc with jacket)
[1. Cave dwellers--Fiction. 2. Prehistoric peoples--Fiction. 3. Alphabet.] I. Title.

PZ7.T6872Cav 2011
[E]--dc22
2010030528

Lot #:
2 4 6 8 10 9 7 5 3 1
03/11
Published by Sterling Publishing Co., Inc.
387 Park Avenue South, New York, NY 10016

www.sterlingpublishing.com/kids

Text and illustrations © 2011 by Janee Trasler
Distributed in Canada by Sterling Publishing
c/o Canadian Manda Group, 165 Dufferin Street
Toronto, Ontario, Canada M6K 3H6
Distributed in the United Kingdom by GMC Distribution Services
Castle Place, 166 High Street, Lewes, East Sussex, England BN7 1XU
Distributed in Australia by Capricorn Link (Australia) Pty. Ltd.
P.O. Box 704, Windsor, NSW 2756, Australia

Printed in China
All rights reserved

Sterling ISBN 978-1-4027-7119-4

For information about custom editions, special sales, premium and
corporate purchases, please contact Sterling Special Sales
Department at 800-805-5489 or specialsales@sterlingpublishing.com.